Ali Bear and the Dragon

By Kyle Spencer
Illustrated by Bruce Winchester

For Esme

Published by
Rabbit and Fox

I was tucking my son into bed one night;
When he said, “Wait! Don’t turn off the light!
To help me sleep,
can you do something for me?
Please can you read me a bedtime story?”

“How about Goldilocks and the three bears?
I’m sure we’ve got the book somewhere.”
“Oh, no!” he replied “Not that book!
That naughty girl - well, she’s a crook!”

“I want a story I’ve not heard before,
Where heroes do battle
and dragons give roar!”
“Are you sure?”

“Yes! Wizards with grey beards
and pointy hats
Versus witches on broomsticks
with their familiar cats!”

“Elves and knights fighting as one
Until a mighty battle is won!”
”I think I’m getting the picture, my son...”

“And fearsome monsters that run on all fours,
With two big heads and
two sets of jaws!”
“Well, I might oblige, if
you would just pause...”

“A castle under siege!
Ruled by the king, the liege!”

“OK! Slow down, my little bear!
Give me a moment to prepare.
Hmm. So, where to begin?
‘Inside a cave, for a dragon lies within ...

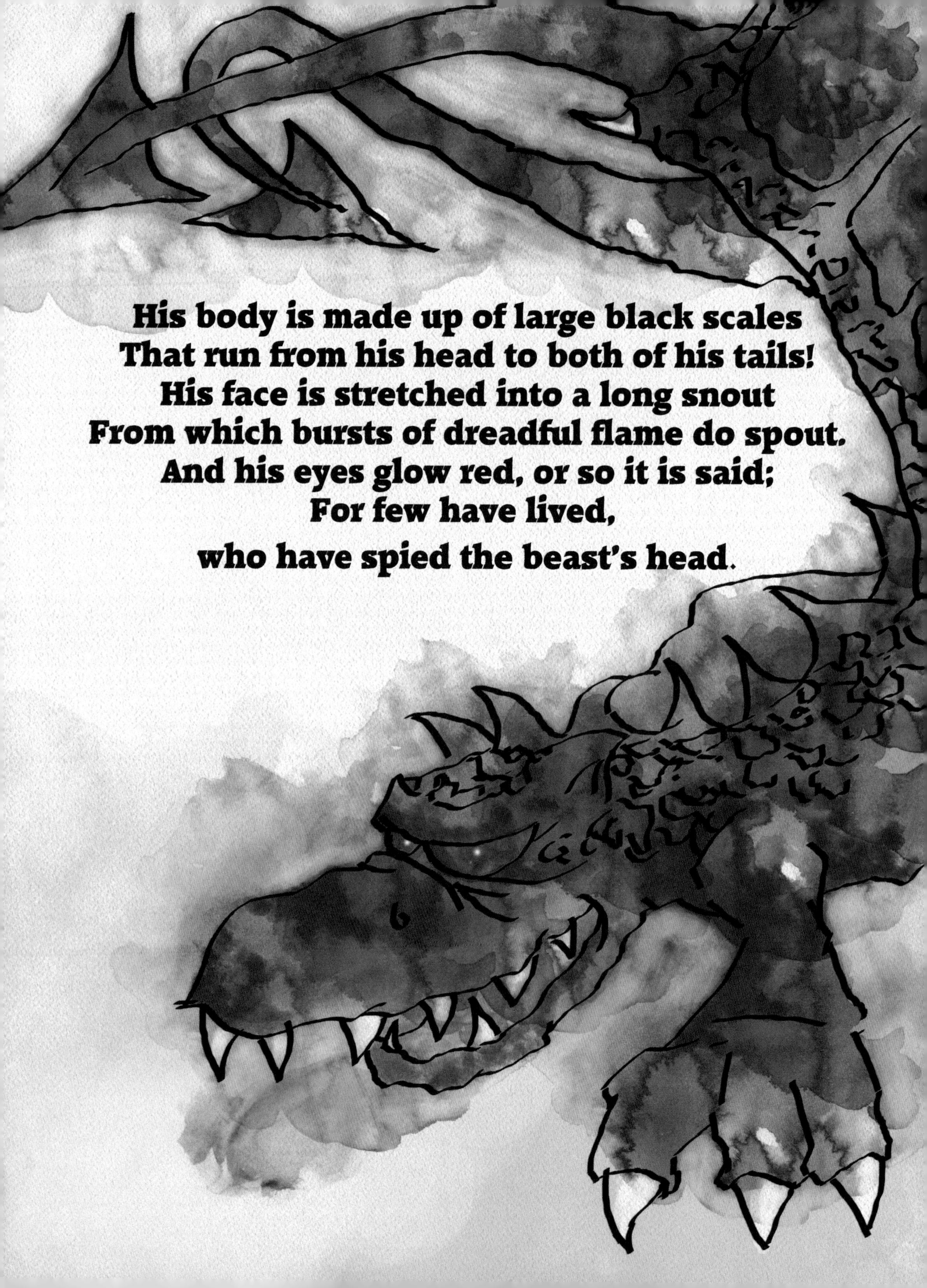

His body is made up of large black scales
That run from his head to both of his tails!
His face is stretched into a long snout
From which bursts of dreadful flame do spout.
And his eyes glow red, or so it is said;
For few have lived,
who have spied the beast's head.

He captured damsels just for fun
Before the end of each day was run;
He loved to burn castles down on sight;
Then snack upon toasted kebab of knight!

Which is why once, a long time ago -
Some ten or twenty years or so -
The king gave a quest to his best hero!
This was the plan - bear with me, it was daft -
For he ordered from his witches
a sleeping draught.

Nothing nasty, you understand;
The witches refused any dastardly plans
Because harming others is against their code,
(Though pointing out warts
still gets you turned into a toad!)

So the brew was to be taken
into the beasts cave
By none other than Sir Bold the Brave!
Then - the best bit, I suppose -
Was he had to pour it down it's nose!
The quest went well, without a care,
But Sir the Bold the Brave
stole the dragon's teddy bear!

So now that the beast is sound asleep,
Let us look at matters away from his keep.

The land was ruled by a king and fair queen,
The people were happy, or so it would seem.
But in the darkest hearts of men,
Amongst monsters foul in secret glens
Trouble was preparing to strike - but when?

You see, wizards are sly
and lustful for power
And had mastered dark arts
ready for the hour
When they would lead an army
to make the land cower!

With a swish of their staff
They summoned on their behalf
Scores of beasts with two heads.
And with a zip and a zap
They woke from his nap
The dragon that everyone dreads.

When conjuring was done,
Tales of spoils of war were spun;
And to the castle they marched in unison.

Oh, wait a minute; I'm ahead of myself,
I forgot to mention the tall, blond elves.
They lived, of course, in Avalon;
But maintained a castle garrison.

Their sharp eyes watching to the east
Were the first to spot approaching beast
Emerging from surrounding wood:
Six feet tall each of them stood!

With two angry heads
and rows of sharp teeth,
With razors for claws,
which they loved to unsheathe.
With bodies covered in thick grey fur,
They surged forwards in a blur!

As fast as a panther, as big as a bear,
These monsters came
from your worst nightmare!
I should also point out
they were smelly too;
Never use the bathroom
after one has been to the loo!

The king gave his orders on the ramparts,
But his first command was not a good start.
In open combat knights
would be sorely tested,
So surely behind castle walls
they couldn't be bested?
But twenty years of being dragon-free
Meant of war the king knew little, you see.

The castle gate flew open across the moat;
"You evil things, you just...get my goat!"
(I know, as one-liners go it was a damp squib,
But the king wasn't very good at doing ad-lib.)
Nevertheless, knights poured out on horse,
Engaging the enemy without remorse!

Arrows flew across the night sky
From elven archers positioned high.
Bowstrings stretched till they were taut,
Then let fly...but all for naught!
For the cowardly wizards hiding behind trees
Used magical spells to turn arrows into peas!

They harmlessly fell on the enemy side
As their mirth the wizards
didn't bother to hide!
The beasts took advantage,
crashing into the knights,
Now, ladies, you should have seen the sight!

For wizards, you see, don't play fair;
They vanished armour revealing underwear!
Brave, macho knights of the kingdom,
you and I might like to think
Well, explain to me, then,
why some wore pink?

The noise was fearsome as claw met shield!
But Sir Marvellous and his banana
were soon forced to yield.
Items were swung and jaws were blocked;
But Sir Dashing was forced to parley
in a fetching frock.
Sir Courageous struck a beast across the head!
Not exactly a mortal blow,
when armed with loaf of bread.
Sir Bold the Brave struck clearly for all to see!
Unfortunately only with
smelly French Brie.

The dull-witted king let out a sigh.
"Huh! At least it can't get worse,"
to his aides he did confide.

From the cave it roared!
And to the sky it soared!
The dragon of terror, awake at last
Hurtled toward the battlefield fast!

**"Unleash the dwarfs!" the king now cried.
"What dwarfs?" his generals asked surprised.
"My liege not all stories
with elves have dwarfs!"
"Oh of course, er, Unleash the witches!"
the king cried out loud;
And before you could say "Which witches?"
they appeared like a cloud.**

A formation of witches, astride broomsticks,
Swept down from the heavens
in attempt to fix,
The magical malady of the knights' jinx.

The witches were old, with poor eyesight;
So they used their cats to navigate in flight;
Accurate they were, I must confess -
Better than Tom-Tom or GPS.

Magic now began to fill the air;
Armour returned to cover derrière,
And mighty carrots were now replaced
By weapons of choice - the sword or the mace!

The witches' cats got involved too,
Firing hair balls
- but let's leave it there, that's just ew!

The cowardly wizards in the trees
Saw it was time to turn, to run, to flee.
And nothing demoralized
their monsters faster,
Than not being able to keep up
with their retreating masters!

The knights, witches
and elves cheered as one
As they thought the battle won.
"Dragooooooon!!!"

The king had finished shouting "Hooray"
When he added,
"I beg your pardon - what did you say?"

The beast landed on his rump,
Before the knights, with a terrifying thump;
All remembered tales, the legends of old
Of the dragons who ate knights - hot, not cold.
As each man fearfully hugged another,
The king he simply squeaked out, "Mother!"

The situation looked increasingly dire
As the dragon opened his mouth to let out...

...

...

"Sire!
I believe a knight took my teddy bear,
But for this, your kingdom I would not spare
But hand him over and I will agree
Not to eat all of you - perhaps two or three?".

Sir Bold the Brave, still armed with cheese,
Flung it at the dragon
(calculating first the cross-breeze);
The dragon's mouth it opened with rage,
Swallowing it whole...
the silence lasted an age.

Eventually he said,
"What's this? It's rather nice.
It doesn't give indigestion
like a knight-pizza slice."

Sir Bold replied, "It's a cheese called Brie."
"Hmm," said the dragon. " It's really tasty."

And so everyone was rather glad
That the dragon of terror preferred salad!

He cleaned up the battlefield buffet;
Whilst everyone cheered (again) "hooray!"
The bear was returned,
to the dragon's delight,
And he waved goodbye
as he took off in flight.

And so, all that it remains to say,
Is that, despite the heroes on display,
It was really the teddy bear
that saved the day!'

Printed in Great Britain
by Amazon